SINK YOUR TEETH INTO CHRISTMAS

Blood and Holly Mayhem!

I0684435

Edited by Dorothy Davies

SINK YOUR TEETH INTO CHRISTMAS

Blood and Holly Mayhem!

GRAVESTONE PRESS

Table of Contents

He's Behind You!

David Turnbull

Christmas Eve, the matinee performance of Aladdin and his Magical Lamp, Bobby Leslie was sweating inside the silky folds of his elaborate Widow Twankey costume. The dress itself weighed a ton. He was feeling his age. His stomach was giving him jip and his gout was playing up.

The stalls were filled with screaming youngsters, dumped there by stressed out mums who were treating the theatre like some sort of glorified crèche while they panicked around the High Street getting their last-minute Xmas shopping. Their kids were hyper on cheap advent calendar chocolate and the promise of what Santa would bring in the morning. The shenanigans which erupted inside the theatre were giving Bobby a banging headache.

"He's behind you!" howled the kids, showering the stage with popcorn and other less savoury missiles.

"Beg your pardon?" said Bobby, cupping a hand over his ear, and fluttering his huge, ridiculously exaggerated eyelashes.

"He's behind you!" came the chaotically boisterous response.

Bobby knew that the young actor playing the role of Aladdin was standing behind him, silently egging on the kids, ready to move in the carefully synchronised manner they'd rehearsed, so that

Bobby wouldn't manage to see him no matter how he turned and turned.

"I can't hear a word you're saying," said Bobby. This part of the panto was mainly ad-lib, depending on the age profile of the audience and what fettle they were in. "I'm looking for my boy, Aladdin," he teased, puckering his apple red lips. "Have any of you lot seen him?"

"He's behind you!" Some of the kids in the front row dramatically rolled their eyes and slapped their brows as if they couldn't believe how dumb he was being.

"Beg pardon," said Bobby, flouncing around with his hand cupped to his ear, as Aladdin crouched low and followed him all around the stage.

"Behind you!"

It was a roar now. Bobby knew the kids had almost reached the limit of their patience. The joke was wearing thin. The whole situation was on a knife edge. If he kept the pretence going much longer, he'd lose them all together.

But Bobby didn't want to turn around. It wasn't just the eager young actor he'd see. There would be something else. Something that had been lurking behind the shoulders of his mirror reflection for days. Something for his eyes only. Something no one else could see. Something ghostly, grotesque, and monstrous.

What made it worse was that Bobby knew exactly who it was.

"Behind you!" yelled the kids.

Bobby felt a bead of sweat go trickling down the inside of his petticoats.

"Behind me, you say?"

The kids roared with laughter. Bobby knew this wasn't for him. It was Aladdin, popping up behind him, pulling faces and making out old Widow Twankey had gone completely loopy. Bobby swung around on the stacked heels of his fancy shoes. He felt Aladdin rushing to hide behind his skirts.

And there he was, in the shadows to the rear of the stage, horribly forlorn in his pale, sad faced Pierrot clown make up. Baggy silk costume all torn and bloody. Mangy pompom buttons drooping on the tunic. Dented conical hat askew on his head. Studs of shattered windscreen crystals sparkling in the innumerate puncture wounds on his face.

Bobby had screamed the first time the corpse clown had materialised in his shaving mirror one morning. Screamed and bit down on his lower lip so hard he tasted blood. Now the scream was internalised. Swallowed to yank like a tight and painful knot in his belly. But no less traumatic in its physical effect.

Surprise, the apparition rasped, grinning like the proverbial wolf in sheep's clothing. Bobby's heart thumped so hard in his chest he thought he was going to have a heart attack. He gulped and turned back to the kids in the audience.

"Whatever are you talking about?" he asked them, struggling against the tremble that wanted to seize his voice. "There's no one there. No one at all."

"He's behind you!" the kids screamed, jabbing sticky doughnut jam index fingers to where, according to what they'd rehearsed, Aladdin kept popping up comically and peeping over Widow Twankey's frilly padded shoulders.

I know he's behind me, thought Bobby but why now? If you're going to haunt someone, why wait twenty years to start? He made to turn in one direction but swung on his heels the opposite way. "There you are," he scolded. "Where have you been, silly boy? There are chores to be done."

Aladdin was caught on the hop. He wasn't supposed to be rumbled quite yet. He almost fluffed his next line but pulled himself together at the last moment.

"Look what I found," he said, holding up his prize.

"Wherever did you get that awful looking lamp?" Bobby wagged a finger. "You ought to throw it out with the rubbish."

"Oh no, Ma," said Aladdin, shaking his head solemnly and clutching the plastic prop that passed for an oil lamp. "Once I polish this up nice and proper, it'll be good as new."

He turned and addressed the audience. "Who knows what might happen if I give it a good rub. Isn't that right, children?"

"That's right!" roared the enthusiastic response.

The panto proceeded. Somehow Bobby managed to make it right through to the singalong ensemble finale without having to glance over his shoulder. But once he got into his dressing room and had to use the mirror to take off the caked layers of make-up, the ghoulish clown was there, right behind him in the reflection.

"What do you want?" he demanded, wiping away rouge with a cotton ball. "And why wait all this time to come and get it?"

Revenge is a dish best served cold, rattled the clown, the crystal studs pocked over his face glinting back the glare from the coloured lights on the dresser.

"I'm not scared of you, Ron," said Bobby, lying through his teeth and trying desperately to hold on to his wits. The horrible entity felt so close that it wasn't hard to imagine its cold breath on the back of his neck. Bobby shivered.

You should be afraid of me, said the wraith. It grinned beneath its tainted greasepaint, revealing an uneven row of yellow, nicotine-stained teeth. *You robbed me of my life and I intend to take something from you in return.*

Bobby wiped away some more of his make-up. "It was an accident, Ron. A tragic accident. There was nothing intentional about what happened."

So said the inquest, came the angry response. *But there was more to what befell me than met the eye. You know that. And I, sure as hell, know that.*

A shiver of a different sort washed over Bobby. How could he know? How could he possibly know? He'd been fast asleep at the time.

***

Christmas Eve two decades earlier,

It was approaching midnight, sleet falling in the car park of a working men's club somewhere in the midlands, when Bobby Leslie and Ron Tozer, each once struggling stand-up comedians in their forties, were heading for the little transit van they used to ferry themselves around the circuit.

They were well past their sell buy date, but were now rising stars as a result of joining forces to create a wholly unique double act as Zingo and Blatt, the inebriated clowns, irreverently bickering and bitching about each other's performances and those of other members. Their imaginary circus troupe had started life as a short sketch for a fringe review at the Edinburgh Festival. The premise had been to pull together half a dozen stand-ups and challenge them to try something new.

Bobby and Ron had come up with the clown idea over a pint. Ron, as Zingo, the straight man, tall and lanky, dressed in the dishevelled Pierrot outfit, Bobby, the funny one, short and squat in an oversized tramp outfit, complete with a red rubber nose, battered bowler hat and startlingly luminous green wig.

The original sketch only ran to ten minutes. They had to fill at least half an hour, sometimes forty-five minutes. They borrowed mercilessly from the greats, padding out their set with stuff from Laurel & Hardy, Morecambe and Wise and the Two Ronnies. Currently their most popular skit was based on Abbot and Costello's legendary *Who's on First?* Theirs was called *Who's Out First?* Instead of a baseball team, Zingo was attempting to explain to an increasingly flabbergasted Blatt the proposed running order of clowns out of an exploding car.

"*Who* comes out first." Zingo would say.

"I don't know," Blatt would reply. "That's why I'm asking you. Who comes out first?"

"Exactly."

"What?"

"Not *What*. *What* comes out second. *Who* comes out first."

"Who?"

"Yes."

"What?"

"Not *What*. He's second. *Who* comes out first."

And so it would go on, back and forth, as the audience howled with laughter.

It had been a hard slog, though. Three solid months on the road takes it out of you. Bobby was looking forward to spending Christmas with his family. His daughter was six and he missed her badly. He was glad there were no more bookings lined up till mid-January.

On the other hand, the coming year was looking very promising in terms of their career trajectory. There was a very real prospect of a Zingo and Blatt sitcom being developed for television. A production company had commissioned a team of writers to devise a plot for a pilot. Bobby and Ron would come up with the gags, the team would embed them within a storyline. If the pitch worked there would be six episodes and an option for a second series if the viewing figures were reasonable.

Ron was already celebrating. He'd necked half a bottle of whisky in the dressing room and Bobby had to hold him by the elbow to keep him steady as they walked through the carpark. Bobby had only drunk a small glass. It was his turn to drive and, with the weather the way it was, he needed to keep his wits about him.

Bobby had changed out of his stage gear, but Ron was still in full regalia, right down to the conical hat perched jauntily on his head and strapped under his chin. "Sod it," he'd said, crammed in the little annex of the club that passed for a dressing room. "I'll have a shower and get changed when I get home. Costume needs to go into the dry cleaners anyway."

With Ron unsteady on his feet and Bobby trying to keep him upright it was if they'd swapped roles. Blatt was now the straight man and Zingo the fool. Bobby thought the contrast might provide some excellent raw material for a scene in the sitcom pilot. Maybe even the opening scene. He made a mental note to recount the incident when the meeting with the writers was scheduled.

By the time Bobby started the van's engine and pulled out of the carpark, Ron was singing White Christmas. He'd always fancied himself as a bit of a crooner. Even drunk and slurring the words he didn't have a bad voice. Bobby thought maybe they could incorporate a song into the act. Ron, as Zingo, plaintively singing a love song. Bobby, as Blatt, irreverently sabotaging the whole affair. That would be a hoot. Audiences would love that. He made another mental note.

The sleet was turning to snow. The streets were hung with multi-coloured fairy lights. They passed the town square, its Christmas tree decked with glassy green and red baubles Bobby felt himself filling up with the joy of the season. In the back of the van was a large parcel containing the doll's house he'd bought as a special gift for his daughter. Life was good and things were set to get even better.

The snow thickened, inspiring him to join Ron on the chorus. He wondered if, next year at this time, a Zingo and Blatt Christmas special might be airing on TV. Wouldn't that be something? He'd heard that they often filmed Christmas shows in June. He chuckled at the notion, taking the roundabout exit for the A road that led toward the motorway.

Ron stopped singing as they headed out of town. He brought the whiskey bottle out of his costume pocket and took another swig. The snow was now blanketing the sides of the road. Bobby switched on his fog lights and increased the speed of the windscreen wipers.

Ron began to snore, mouth wide as he slouched in the passenger seat, a film of drool oozing from the side of his mouth, cutting a raggedy channel through the white powder on his face. In the years that followed Bobby went over what he did next a billion times and still couldn't fathom what had possessed him to do such a reckless thing as unbuckle Ron's seatbelt.

He recalled chuckling to himself. *That'll teach him. Next bend I take he'll get slammed into the door. That'll wake the drunken bugger up.*

How was he to know that the sleet on the road at the next bend had already frozen to black ice? How was he to know that the sheet of snow covering it would make it even more treacherous?

Before he knew it, he was steering into a skid that became a hair raising, gut churning spin.

The van left the road and trundled violently down an embankment. Ron cried out in shock as he was tossed around without the restraint of the seatbelt. There came an almighty crash as the van hit a tree. Bobby felt his head jerk back. He momentarily lost consciousness as the air bag inflated.

A minute or so later he came around to the sound of the engine droning and the acrid smell of smoke filling his nostrils. When he looked to the passenger seat it was empty. Ahead of him the windscreen was smashed out. Smoke was billowing from the buckled bonnet.

Groggily, he stepped out into the snow.

"Ron?" he called into the gathering blizzard. "Ron? Are you ok, mate?"

No reply.

The cold and the shock caused Bobby to shiver uncontrollably.

Then he saw Ron, sprawled awkwardly on the snowy slope of the embankment, face bloodied and studded with the glass crystals of the shattered windscreen, make up horrifically smeared, staring back at him through cold, dead eyes.

***

Those same eyes stared at him now. He was in the back seat of a taxi, travelling home for an early dinner with his wife before the evening performance. He could see Ron/Zingo in the

16

driver's mirror. Those dreadful eyes, bloodshot and full of pent-up ire.

Make sure no one sneakily undoes your seatbelt, he rasped menacingly at Bobby's ear.

"You do that radio show, don't you?" said the taxi driver. "The one where you play all those novelty songs?"

"I do," said Bobby. This was the niche career he'd managed to build for himself after the accident. He'd become quite an authority on the novelty song.

"My old man loves that show," said the taxi driver. "Reminds him of his childhood."

"There's a lot of nostalgia in those old songs," agreed Bobby, glad of the conversation and trying to avoid looking in the mirror.

"Who's the geezer who sings about his boomerang not coming back?"

"Charlie Drake," said Bobby.

"That it," said the taxi driver. "He's in that book you wrote."

"Agadoo to Zenga Zenga, the A to Z of the Novelty Song," said Bobby, feeling quite proud of himself. The book had been out for five years and was still selling quite well, especially at Christmas when people hankered for a bit of frivolity. A couple of years back he'd even had a little slot on the One Show to talk about some of the songs featured in it.

"I got that book for my old man's birthday last year," said the taxi driver. "If I'd have known you'd be in the back of my cab I'd have brought it with me and asked you to sign it for him."

"If he's local we could probably come to some arrangement," said Bobby.

"Really?" said the taxi driver.

"I could meet him at the theatre café, or he could come to the radio station," suggested Ron. "If he brings the book, I'll sign it. It would me my pleasure."

"Oh boy," said the taxi driver. "You wait till I tell him. It'll make his day. He hasn't been well recently."

"Glad to be of help," said Bobby.

In the mirror Ron Tozer's ghostly image rolled its eyes as if it was thoroughly disgusted by the notion.

***

"Hey, Angie, I'm back," called Bobby as he hung his coat in the hallway.

His wife called back from the kitchen. "Just a second."

Bobby went into the downstairs toilet. The wan faced Pierrot stared at him from the mirror above the sink. *Murdered by a practical joke,* said Ron, scowling over his shoulder.

"I'm sorry," said Bobby. "I truly didn't intend you any harm."

It's not the intention that matters, said Ron. *It's the end result. Think where our careers might have gone if you hadn't been so cruel and reckless?*

"You think I don't realise that?" asked Bobby. "You think I haven't been filled with regret for the past twenty years?"

But you never confessed, did you? challenged Ron. *When the police asked you about my seatbelt, you lied. You said I was drunk and probably didn't notice that it wasn't clipped in properly.*

"How do you know all this?" demanded Bobby.

When you spend a long time in limbo, you see things, said Ron. *Certain facts get revealed to you. Certain events leading to your demise become clear.*

"So why now?" asked Bobby again. "Why wait till now?"

Ron tapped the side of his powdered nose and gave a sly wink of his eye. *All will be revealed in good time. Don't you worry about that. A while ago something roused me. So here I am, ready for my curtain call.*

Bobby heard the creak of a floorboard outside in the corridor. He flushed the toilet and opened the door. Angie was there in her apron, sleeves rolled up on her blouse. "Were you talking to yourself in there?"

"Just rehearsing a new gag I'm thinking of slipping into the show," said Bobby, covering his tracks.

"As long as you're not getting all morbid," said Angie. "I know this time of the year is difficult. Because of … well you know…"

"I'm fine," said Bobby, feeling far from fine. "The little 'un will be here tomorrow. I'm really looking forward to it." Their granddaughter, Claire, was fourteen months old. She was going to be able to appreciate Christmas much better than last year, when she was just a babe at arms.

"I spoke to Debs earlier," said Angie. "They're going to set off around nine. All being well they'll be here just after eleven in the morning. The turkey is already defrosting."

"Anything I can do?" asked Bobby.

Angie shook her. "It's all in hand. How was the matinee?"

"Hell on earth," said Bobby.

"Kids?" said Angie.

"Screaming hordes of them," said Bobby, shaking his head wearily.

"Oh dear," said Angie. "And another show tonight. Go soak yourself in a hot bath. I've got your favourite for dinner."

"Ham, eggs and chips?" asked Bobby hopefully.

Angie smiled. "You got it, buster."

Bobby kissed her on the forehead and said the little affectionate words he'd said to her so often over the years. "Angela, you're my angel."

She chuckled. "Don't go getting carried away. Tomorrow morning, I will be truly demonic. Literally cracking the whip. There's going to spuds to peel, sprouts to cross, stuffing to be mixed."

"'Tis the season to be jolly," Bobby responded.

"Off you go and run your bath then," said Angie. "I'll get the chips on."

If only she knew your dirty little secret, Ron's voiced came rasping malevolently into his ear.

***

Bobby preferred the evening performances. More adults in the audience. He could litter his lines with saucy innuendo. The mums and dads would hoot and howl as he winked knowingly back at them. Laughter was contagious. The kids would laugh along not even knowing what the joke was.

He managed somehow to avoid looking directly behind him for the entire performance. Even during his little synchronised sequence with Aladdin, he managed to relegate Ron's dreadful spectre to his peripheral vision, thus avoiding having to look his straight in his gory, glass studded face.

But he couldn't avoid seeing him in the dressing room mirror, or the driver's mirror in the taxi home, or the mirror in the bathroom, or the full-length one in the bedroom, grinning in his awful, smeared make-up, revealing his tobacco yellowed teeth. He was like the shadow of Bobby's shameful past, endlessly trailing behind him.

That night he couldn't avoid the sense that Ron, in the persona of Zingo, was lurking in the shadows of the bedroom as Angie snored gently next to him. Couldn't avoid the soul-destroying sense of guilt he felt for his stupid seatbelt prank two decades earlier. Couldn't avoid wondering just what it was Ron had in store for him. Couldn't close his eyes. Couldn't sleep.

Couldn't get the kids' voices out of his head.
He's behind you!
He's behind you!
Frozen to the spot, afraid to roll over, because he knew Zingo would be there, yellow teeth beneath

21

a bloody red grin, he lay, eyes wide, till the early hours.

***

Christmas Day. Bobby felt exhausted, bleary eyed, washed out. He cut his finger while peeling the potatoes. The plaster wrapped around the wound was making the preparation of the sprouts take forever. Angie was bustling around, swathed in steam from various items simmering on the hob, singing along to the Christmas songs on the radio, frequently getting the lyrics wrong, as she always did.

In the wee small hours Bobby had contemplated making a confession, just sitting down with her over coffee, heaving a big sigh, then pouring his heart out about what he'd done all those years back. Maybe that was what Ron wanted. Wasn't it a thing with ghosts? They hung around because there was unfinished business? Maybe Bobby's concealing of the truth was Ron's *unfinished* business? If he confessed, might he get Ron off his back?

When it came to it, he couldn't bring himself to speak the words. They'd been stuck in his throat ever since he'd lied when the police asked why Ron's seatbelt wasn't fastened. Besides, this wasn't a good day for any of that. Angie was so excited about their daughter, son-in-law and granddaughter coming for Christmas lunch. How could he spoil it? How, on this day of all days, how could he say to his wife, *you know the man who you consider to be a good husband, father and grandfather? Well, he harbours a terrible secret. There's blood on his hands and the ghost of a dead man lurking at his back.*

He finished off the sprouts and glanced at the kitchen window. Zingo grinned menacingly from behind his reflection, the studs of glass crystals like frosty dew on the cold face of a corpse. *Revenge will be mine,* Ron's voice whispered into his ear.

"Are you okay?" asked Angie. "You've gone pale as a sheet."

Bobby smiled at her. "Just tired. Those back-to-back performances took it out of me. Not as young as I used to be."

"Go put your feet up and see what's on TV," she told him. "Everything's on the go now."

"What about the stuffing?" he asked, feeling guilty.

"Done before you were out of bed," she said.

"Angela you are an..."

"I know. I know," she said, shooing him off. "Get some rest. You'll need all your energy for your granddaughter. She loves all her grandad's attention."

Bobby slumped down into the armchair and picked up the remote control. For a moment before he switched on the TV the Pierrot grinned back at him from the blank screen.

***

The ringing of the doorbell and the sound of voices in the hallway roused him from his sleep. His

23

neck felt stiff. He wiped drool from his chin. The Wizard of Oz was showing on TV, the scene where Dorothy first encounters the Scarecrow.

A weary Bobby rose to his feet. His knees cracked.

"Merry Christmas," said a voice from the living room doorway.

His son in law stood there with Bobby's granddaughter perched in his arms. She looked very Christmassy. Little red velvet dress. Red ribbon in her hair. Angie was going have a field day taking snaps of her opening the presents from under the tree then posting them on Facebook.

"Hey there poppet," said Bobby. "How's Claire, my cuddly bear?"

Usually, his granddaughter would have had her arms outstretched as soon as she set eyes on him. But not today. Today she howled as soon as he took a step toward her. Her eyes went wide as saucers. Her scream pierced at his ears. She buried her head in her father's chest.

"She's tired," apologised his son in law. "She was up early."

"What's all the commotion?" asked Angie, entering the room with Debs following behind. Debs took her daughter in her arms, held her tight and patted her back. "It's only grampa," she cooed. "You like grampa. He's always teaching you those silly songs of his."

Claire raised her head and turned slightly. Then she saw Bobby, and let out another strangled howl. She clung desperately to her mother's neck, sobbing uncontrollably. Bobby knew in that instant what

24

was causing her distress. She could see Ron behind him, in the persona of the ghoulish Pierrot, face studded with windscreen crystals. He remembered Debs as a little girl saying how creepy uncle Ron looked when he dressed up a Zingo.

Joke's on you, pal, Ron's voice breathed as his ear. *I get to choose who can see me. You like the punchline?*

So this was it. This was Ron's revenge. He'd said he'd take something from Bobby in return for the loss of his life. Bobby felt as if he'd been punched hard in the gut. Ron was taking the most precious thing he possibly could from Bobby, his relationship with his granddaughter.

It had been Claire's birth that had roused him and provided his potential route to vengeance. Once Ron had become conscious of her, he'd had to wait till he was sure she'd be conscious of him. Now he was well and truly centre stage. She'd never want to go near Bobby so long as she could see Zingo's ghostly countenance at his shoulder.

In sheer desperation he tried singing *My Boomerang Won't Come Back*, adopting that Charlie Drake whinny Cockney voice that made Claire giggle. Last time he'd done this she'd actually shrieked with delight. Now she took one look and shrieked in terror.

You know what she's saying, don't you? mocked Ron, humming like a malicious fly at his ear. *The exact thing she'll be saying till the day you die.*

Bobby stopped singing. His hands were trembling. A tear ran down his cheek.

He's behind you, screeched Ron. *That's what she's saying. He's behind you! He's behind you! He's behind you!*

And he laughed and laughed and laughed as Bobby's granddaughter screamed and screamed and screamed and another Christmas went up in ashes.

God Rest Ye, Merry

Liam A. Spinage

Meredith stood at the gates of Newfield Lodge, transfixed by the view through the flurry of snow which peppered the pathway to the great house itself. At her feet lay her paisley patterned holdall, bulging at what seams remained with all the trappings she thought she would need for the Christmas weekend. The holdall had seen better days, but not so Meredith. Though her face was flush with the cold, her body remained as limber as it had been in her youth when she had lived here.

The lodge had seen better days too, she thought. Whilst there had evidently been some efforts made to maintain the garden and keep the undergrowth from encroaching on the driveway, she could tell from this distance the house itself had aged in those intervening years. Even through the light snowfall and the great gasps of misty breath issuing from her into the chilly evening air, she could spot a chimney high above that needed pointing, three boarded up windows and the overgrown curve of the path which led behind the facade of the lodge proper to access what they had always called the east wing.

They had always referred to it as the east wing, she realised, even though it was neither a wing of the lodge - having an entirely separate entrance hidden from the view of visitors by a grove of elm -

or indeed located to the east. Its westbound entrance meant it got very little light early in the morning which ensured that the servants it once housed had to rely on a series of gongs and bells to awaken from their slumber and begin preparations to serve the family. And what preparations there were - work began early in the kitchen and the scullery for breakfast, with cook often choosing to sleep in the kitchen itself to keep the fires burning low overnight, while the family began their daily activities. An army of scullery maids, butlers, cooks, cleaning dailies, valets, maids and household managers went about their business silent and invisible to them.

She wondered idly if the old man would be there. Surely he must have passed on by now, though she had heard no gossip to that end. A chill passed through her as she contemplated that. She couldn't recall any pleasant memories of the esteemed patriarch's near-tyrannical rule of the place. Most of the family avoided him whenever possible and many of the staff did likewise. But they had enjoyed themselves here, she remembered with a smile. Yes, there had been good times between the wars when the place would often throng with weekend parties. Good times indeed.

She puffed warm breath on her hands to warm up – and she had somehow neglected her gloves in packing - Meredith began to crunch her way down the driveway, lost in thought. So lost in fact that it almost came as a surprise to her when she stood before the imposing double doors, still formidable in their polished oak with the iron clasps only showing a few signs of rust. Here and there on the steps up there were a few flecks of snow and ice but it was clear someone else was already here and had thoughtfully swept aside what had managed to accumulate on the cold grey flagstones so as not to inconvenience the guests.

What guests, though? Meredith had been surprised to receive an invitation to spend the weekend at the old place - at Christmas of all times! It had been many years since she'd set foot here or heard from anyone else. While she maintained to herself that it was curiosity which compelled her to reply in the positive, she also had to contend with the fact that it was really loneliness that had been the overriding imperative. Had she other invitations to spend the holidays, she might have forsaken this one in favour of a less bothersome journey.

Still, old acquaintances waited within, presumably. There were no other footprints in the snow on the drive, she noticed, and no sign of any vehicles. She wondered idly who, then, had swept the stair. Maybe some of the old staff still worked here, kept the place going? Interesting.

Smiling to herself as if she had discovered some important clue (Meredith often imagined herself as some dedicated lady sleuth laying bare the iniquities of ne'er-do-wells throughout the English countryside), she tentatively reached forward to ring the bell-pull, only to find the door already slightly ajar. As if uttering a last gasp, the hinges groaned as she pushed, just as a gust caught her unawares from behind as if to hurry her in.

Behind her, beyond the hedge and unseen even by her keen eyes, a figure stood, solid and silent, watching as the door closed behind her and she finally entered the lodge proper.

Meredith emerged from the atrium into the great hall and deposited the heavy holdall at the foot of the stairway. She looked up at its great spiral through three floors of splendour, still bedecked with portraiture of the estate lineage, moustachioed and bearded and all. Their piercing eyes seemed to judge her as she shook the powder from her coat and laid it to rest on an ancient teak side table easily as old as the old pile itself.

The hall retained none of its warmth, being largely a cold and draughty room through which people passed rather than dwelt. Someone had been busy making it look festive, though - a great fir stood tall at the north end, bedecked in homemade decorations of the kind they had fashioned themselves when young. A great wreath of holly and ivy took pride of place in the little table in the middle of the hall, so much so that even though it was propped up by a stand it looked like it was about to lurch forward unexpectedly and hurtle pell-mell to the chessboard marble of the floor.

The stairs had been decorated with strings of hellebore, their pastel pinks speckled with violet. They gave off a sweet, welcoming fragrance which made a firm change from the damp earth in the grounds. Meredith leaned forward to inhale deeper.

"Winter rose."

Meredith nearly tumbled forward and lost her balance, steadying herself on the banister rail at the last moment.

"Sorry! A mop of unruly brown hair emerged from a door frame deep in one of the hall recesses. "Didn't mean to give you a fright."

"Well, a fright is what you gave me, meant or otherwise." Meredith rallied herself and turned to look at the approaching figure, clad as it was in a plain white shirt unbuttoned at the top and casual slacks spotted with white powder. She struggled momentarily to recall, as if a veil still stood between the years spent her in the past and her present incursion into those memories which floated around her like elusive ghosts. It was only when she saw his face that she let her guard down a little. That smile could still captivate her, it seems.

"James!"

"Hello there, Merry." James crossed the hall in great strides, eager to greet her. "It's still sound to call you Merry, is it?" The inquiry seemed genuine, as if he knew already that she'd had little reason to be merry these past years.

"Merry is fine." She allowed herself a little smile, which then rapidly grew into a beam, and permitted a warm hug which lingered between them, not overlong as to be unseemly, but long enough to convey the warmth of feelings once between them. She withdrew momentarily from his embrace to glance at that face. It seemed to Meredith that James had not aged at all. The brash confidence of that boyish smile fair swept her away as she lost herself in the better memories of Newfield.

"Merry Christmas! I was hoping you'd come, more than anyone else."

"Why, you charmer!" Meredith flushed momentarily. "I see you haven't changed much."

"Oh, you know me..." James ran his hand absently through his hair in one of his failed attempts to tame it,

"Well, I dare say I do not after all this time! We shall have to have a proper catch up. Is anyone else here? Who else was invited? I'm not quite sure how or why..."

A gravelly cough behind her gave her a second startle,

"Reckon as how I'd spoil the moment."

If James hadn't changed at all, the same could not be said for the groundskeeper, Chris. Crows' feet radiated from the corners of his small grey eyes and gave way to salt-and-pepper hair receding to a weather-beaten scalp.

"Well!" Meredith composed herself. "Another surprise. I expect this weekend will be full of them."

Chris lurched in closer, clearly slowing with age and favouring a good left leg. From his clasped hands he produced a single winter rose which he offered to Meredith with a slight nod of his head.

"I'm not much of one for hugging, but I'll offer this instead. They grow all over the back of the estate these days. It'll be a fine match for your dress."

"Thank you." Genuinely touched, but a little overwhelmed at all the sudden company after such time without it, Meredith took the flower into her hand. "Well, then, what other surprises are in store for us?"

"Just me, I'm afraid."

All their heads turned this time and gazed up at the great stair. Descending them was another familiar face, attached to an ample frame which one might imagine belonged to a maiden aunt of the sort that kept cats or birds beyond count.

"At least as far as I'm aware."

"Ginny!" It had taken Meredith a moment - again - to recognise that face. Why did memories have to fight their way through the fog of years so? "Are you the last of our company, then?"

"I'm afraid so. No-one else answered the call, it seems." She shrugged, which caused her scarf to become momentarily dislodged and caught in the balustrade. Bearing this unwarranted hiccup with good humour, Virginia reached the bottom stair. There was a brief but warm hug between them which was interrupted by James.

"Let's go through to the kitchens. It's much warmer there and Merry here is still freezing from her trip."

"The kitchens?" Meredith paused, Something wasn't quite right. "But surely,.."

"No point standing on ceremony. There's only us here. We shall have to fend for ourselves. Worry not, I'm quite the dab hand." He gave her a knowing wink.

"Then the old man,,," Meredith spoke barely above a whisper and allowed herself to tail off her own thought, but Ginny ran with it and replied for her.

"Gone, Dead and gone these many years, no more's the pity." Meredith detected a scowl crack across the smooth alabaster of Virginia's face.

For a moment no one spoke. Meredith had perhaps expected one of the men to react at this breach of politeness, but it seems they were in agreement.

"Well, I shan't lose any sleep over him. Good riddance to bad blood, I say!" She took Meredith's arm and led them both down a long oak-panelled corridor to the rear of the hall. After exchanging glances, the men followed.

"She really doesn't know?" This was from James and uttered to Chris alone as they dawdled behind the women.

"She really doesn't. That's why I called you all here, to lay this business to rest for all time."

James nodded, still uncomprehending, as they caught up and all four of them entered the kitchens.

When James had implied he was a dab hand, that had been an understatement. Meredith opened the kitchen door and heady aromas began to vie for dominance in her nostrils. A heavy fragrance of cinnamon and clove from a simmering pot of mulled wine, the warm fruit of a great pudding steaming on the stove, the armfuls of fresh greens waiting to go on the hob, the delicious familiarity of a goose in the oven. Beyond those smells, a great fire burned high in the hearth such that the contrast between the chill of the great hall and the warmth of the kitchens could not be more noticeable.

Meredith sat with Virginia, who had favoured them both with a glass of the mulled wine and opposite Chris who had opened a bottle of brown ale with his knife and leaned back on the chair with his feet on the table. James busied himself with the last preparations for their Christmas feast but kept an eye and ear open on the conversations behind him.

"Oh, you must remember, Merry! It was always around Christmas that the old tyrant got so cranky. We were sure he'd be visited by ghosts himself one of those nights, just like in the story.

James had been half asleep on duty *as usual*"- the mock scold elicited a roaring laugh from James - "and we played a little joke. He ended up simply covered in flour - head to toe - and when the old man saw him I thought he was going to drop dead there and then!" Ginny continued to laugh but Meredith, who had been quietly smiling along with her, suddenly stopped.

"Merry?" Virginia looked concerned. "What is it?"

"It's just that,,," she sighed. "I don't remember. I can recall that we had good times here, despite the old man and his constant demands, but when I try to remember anything specific, I find that I can't. Isn't it odd?"

Chris gazed intently, continuing to drink but said nothing. Virginia reached over and placed a reassuring hand over Meredith's, who managed a small smile at her even as a tear formed in the corner of her eye.

"Thank you. I don't know why this is so difficult. I really don't. If I can ask..." here she paused to drain her glass. "How did the old man die in the end?"

Chris slammed his empty bottle down on the table, causing both the ladies to jump out of their skins. He opened his mouth, about to say something when James interrupted cheerily.

"Dinner is served! Let's have it in here, for old time's sake."

"What do you mean?" Meredith was dizzy now, her head swirling sick not just with the cloying wine but with a heady anticipation that she was about to hear something from their past which would blow away all the fog in her mind.

"I mean, like we celebrated Christmas in the old days before the tragedy. Remember? We'd always have our meal late Christmas Eve, with old master Kettle playing the fiddle while we sipped at the punch and opened our presents. It was always too busy on the day itself, with all the work involved in serving the family in their festivities."

Meredith shook with trepidation. Something formed at the back of her mind, beating on her brain as it struggled to form on her tongue.

"We were the staff? That's..."

"Whoa, quick, catch 'er!" Chris stood quickly, but not quick enough.

Virginia leapt over, just in time to catch Meredith as she slipped from her chair into a stupor.

"Darnit! I knew this'd be too much for her in one night." Chris swore as he strode across to open the door.

The last thing Meredith remembered that evening was James carrying her to bed, Virginia pacing just behind.

"Were? We are the staff. Welcome back, Meredith. Welcome home."

Though sleep came to Meredith swiftly, it was not restful. The fire in her room, warming at first, became all-consuming as it burned fiercer and fiercer behind the grate. Even in the dead of winter, it was uncomfortably warm and Meredith threw off her covers to cool herself down.

Then she screamed.

Under the covers with her was a single white winter rose. Not the gift Chris had given her, which still rested on her dress discarded over a footstool, but one freshly-cut. As she withdrew from the bed, the covers themselves contorted into a full bloom of hellebore, encircling the whole frame and flowing free across the floor to the fire. She stared on in disbelief, still screaming at the top of her voice, when the fire roared up and swallowed the trail of flowers whole. The bed was now on fire, so Meredith tried to run from the room. The door was locked. She tugged at it hopelessly, turning the knob, pulling the handle with all her might, even ringing the bell next to it. As she was about to pass out from the heat, the fire licking at the hem of her nightdress, she heard movement and shouting on the other side. Moments later, James stood there, shirtless and breathless, the door off its hinges. But then he stood and did nothing, just looking at her quizzically.

"James, help!"

"What is it?"

"What? What do you mean, what is it?" She pushed past him into the corridor, eager to escape the inferno, as he watched in alarm.

"Merry! Merry, calm down!"

"How can I calm down when my room's on fire?"

James looked into the room. Merry looked back. There was no fire, not even in the fireplace. A single beam of moonlight shone through the drapes, perfectly illuminating the single hellebore on her dress. Merry, destroyed with grief, suddenly remembered. Waves of memories washed over her, each causing a flood of tears as she stood shivering, openly weeping now in James' embrace.

She stood in the garden the next morning. Chris had shown her where to find it. A single, low grave, fashioned from a crude stone and with a simple engraving. It was hidden at the rear of the east wing which had once served as their quarters, she would never have managed to find it herself even if she had known it was there.

It was Virginia, not James who stood beside her here while she wept and laid a single flower upright at the base of the headstone.

ROSE HELLEBORE WINTERS
1922 TO 1938

"I remember now, I think, I remember it all,"

She turned to regard her, instead Ginny reached out her hands, which Merry grasped.

"It was him, wasn't it? The old man?"

Virginia held back tears of her own. "It was. What do you remember?"

"I remember she was young. I remember he lusted for her. Wanted a little Christmas present from her. I remember I went over your head and shouted at him to leave her alone. I was furious when I found out. Unconstrained."

Virginia hung her head.

"She wasn't the first, was she?"

Virginia shook her head. The tears came unchecked to both of them. "I'm sorry. We're all sorry. We should have done more to help,"

"I understand, I think. I don't want to, but I do. Why bring me back now, though? Why have me remember?"

"It's time to move on, Merry. For all of us to move on. You know yourself that you haven't been able to, not really, until you remember."

"I think I see your point. Well, some Christmas this is turning out to be!" She was almost laughing through the tears now, hysterically. Virginia let the moment pass. "Shall we go back to the others?"

"There's one more thing."

"One more?"

Virginia looked over at her, judging the state of her well-being.

"Two." The admission came with a blush.

"You asked a question last night.. Can you answer it now?"

"The old man. I did it, didn't I? I killed him with my own hands." She looked down at them, not in shame but in incredulity.

Virginia nodded.

"You said there were two things?"

"Look up."

Meredith raised her head high and craned her neck to look up at the east wing. Where once there had been a large building - thought nowhere near as large as the great lodge itself, there was only a ruin now. How had she not noticed this the night before when she had arrived? She struck a foot forward in tentative exploration. The charred remains of beams crushed into ash beneath her feet.

"What happened?" She knew this had to be linked to her sister somehow. She'd recalled everything else now - the good times and the bad - all those merry Christmastides they'd spent together playing and dancing and eating once the household had gone to sleep. All the arguments and staff rivalries. Her bitter condemnation of the lascivious old patriarch. But not this.

"He came looking for you both later. His rage consumed this place. We were in the servants' hall at the rear, before the great fire, roasting chestnuts."

She knew now. Knew what was coming next.

"He fell in."

"You pushed him in. We all saw. None of us stopped you."

"And then?"

"You know. Even in that state, he righted himself. You knocked him back again, but not before the fire caught hold of you too. Caught hold of the building itself. Too fast, too furious. There was no escape. No escape…"

Meredith looked down again, Behind her sister's grave, there was something else. She parted the shrubbery and knelt to rub snow from the stone.

MEREDITH "MERRY" WINTERS
1920 - 1938
DEVOTED SISTER

She looked back at Ginny for the last time. "Everyone?" she asked.

"Everyone but Chris. He slept in the gatehouse."

"Then we're…" She didn't finish. Didn't need to. It explained it all: why no one else had been invited, why there was no trace of their arrival, why none of them looked a day older.

The two of them stood there in the early morning light, James joined them in grief and silence. They looked at each other and slowly, very slowly, began to fade from each other's view.

Behind them all, a pair of eyes surveyed them from the undergrowth, tears swelling in the corners. Chris stood watching until there was no more to see.

"God Rest Ye, Merry."

An Urchin's Christmas

Dan Allen

Cyrus crossed the muddy field, crawling on hands and knees and staying downwind from the rabbit. Like all young boys, his appetite was insatiable. The rabbit stopped its incessant nibbling and froze. Perhaps it sensed danger, but it was too late. The boy was within striking distance and he pounced with the speed and ferocity of a coyote. Cyrus's untamed nails made his three fingers look much longer than usual and he used these knife-like appendages to rip the animal apart. Brilliant red blotches splattered on the pure white-as-snow fur and the urchin paused a moment before sinking in his yellow teeth. Then, after only a bite or two, Cyrus was finished. Apparently he was not as hungry as assumed, or maybe the thrill alone was enough to satisfy his appetite. He stroked the rabbit's soft fur and then dragged the carcass by the ears like a stuffed toy.

The weather was changing and his bare shoulders felt the chill. He moved closer to home and burrowed into a pile of soggy leaves. The ground was damp and the air smelled earthy. Dark skies loomed except for a small ribbon of grey in the west. Hunger pains once again throbbed in his abdomen and he sniffed the air. A woman approached from the bottom of the hill. She looked weighed down by bags and packages, some colourfully wrapped in red and gold.

Dried blood and dirt crumbled beneath the urchin's fingernails and the filthy boy held back a sneeze. He wiped his nose with the back of his hand and snuffed in the rest.

The woman may have heard his animal-like snort. She paused and looked behind, but the sidewalk was empty and she shrugged. Despite the frosty air, it wasn't cold enough for ice, yet the woman gingerly selected each step.

The urchin smiled and his eyes lit like embers stoked by a breeze. Fragile older women were a delicacy. Their flesh, no longer young and firm, had aged to perfection.

Cyrus rose silently and crouched behind a hedge. Always just a shadow behind, he followed her to the top where the streetlights ended and the ancient laneway to Mortaki's mansion began. The urchin tried to be patient, but that was a quality not expected of a child. Instead, he danced from foot to foot as if he had to pee. Finally, the woman must have sensed his presence because she picked up her pace. Streetlights flickered and the wind fell silent.

The boy emerged before her like a magician's trick. He could feel her eyes on him, taking in his long dirty hair, filthy stained skin and the burlap bag he wore like a dress. Then she appeared to notice the rabbit, for her eyes widened with a flash of fear, or perhaps it was confusion.

"Hey, it's too chilly to be walking around with bare feet. You're going to catch a cold, kid." The woman sounded legitimately concerned but kept her distance.

The urchin slowly raised a hand with its three equally long fingers and smiled. A small gust ruffled his hair. Swirling leaves and the smell of rotting apples followed.

"I'm serious, kid. Where do you live? I'll walk you home."

Cyrus pointed to the mansion at the top of the hill and then began taking exaggerated steps backwards. He smiled again and this time his lips curved away from his rotting yellow teeth. He was easily outpacing her.

"Hey, kid, wait up. I need to speak with your parents." She lunged for the boy, but he fled, darting up the hill and dissipating into the night. His laughter trailed, forced and exaggerated, bouncing from one side of the street to the other until it, too, faded away.

'Disappearing' was a trick he practised and he really hadn't gone that far. He waited behind a tree and watched the first snowflake fall. Pains rolled through his body and his stomach growled. He was hungry again and could smell the woman's scent - a delicious mixture of faked confidence and sincere curiosity. He risked a peek from behind the tree and unintentionally made eye contact. Now that she saw him, the jig was up.

The urchin galloped the first few strides, running on all fours, then launched himself. The woman screamed and dropped her packages. She turned to run, but his teeth easily penetrated her coat and sank into her shoulder. Next, a three-fingered

44

hand reached into her hair and pulled back her forehead, exposing her neck. A sharp-pointed fingernail pierced the carotid artery and blood spurted like a hallway water fountain. The urchin bathed himself in the flow, cupped handfuls through his hair and washed his face in crimson. His abnormally long tongue lashed out and licked the blood from around the woman's dimming eyes. Finally the last flicker of life escaped from his trophy and melted like a snowflake against his burning flesh.

Cyrus screeched and howled like a monster in heat. He pounded his chest and then used the woman's own blood to paint her face—lipgloss and eyeshadow in a matching shade. When satisfied with his work, he carried the woman's body deep into the forest behind the master's home and stuffed her in a burrow beneath the roots of a giant maple. She would be safe there in his secret place, but for now, playtime was over and the boy needed to go home.

Cyrus had ventured beyond the confining walls of the mansion and, by doing so, broken the rules. However, he hoped there would be no punishment tonight, no scolding or beatings. Cyrus learned years ago to put away his playthings and as long as he did that, Mortaki would be merciful.

But Mortaki was dead. His bones still lay on the sofa where he'd collapsed shortly after Halloween. Yet somehow the fear he instilled while alive continued to control Cyrus. The boy remembered the weight of the chains and the cramped cages no bigger than a lobster trap. The whip's sting remained as fresh as the welts and scars.

Cyrus paused and tried to understand. His master called him a monster, an animal. He said he was an abomination in the eyes of God, whatever that meant. Cyrus knew about killing, that much was for sure, but he couldn't seem to grasp the concept of death, the idea that his master was never coming back. The boy stared at the grey winter sky and hissed. Finally, he snapped his head to each side until it cracked. Then he crouched low and ran home.

***

Cyrus slipped through the massive double French doors and boldly entered the mansion. He took his time and lit candles along the way. Here there were no Christmas decorations or festive lights. Mortaki had watched his pennies and saved electricity for emergencies. Christmas was a waste of money, only fools would indulge in giving gifts when no profit would follow.

At the bottom of the grand staircase stood the ghost of an elderly man. The phantom came dressed in a tailed tuxedo with a maroon ascot in place of a tie and a black top hat. His white hair cascaded over his shoulders and his long arms bent back awkwardly at the elbows. Mortaki was tall and even in death, he hovered over Cyrus like a praying mantis.

Cyrus raised his forearm like a shield and coward on his knees.

"You know the rules, son. You'll spend the night in chains for this," Mortaki's ghost spoke with the same dull, scolding tone as the man himself used while alive.

Cyrus bowed his head. "Please... No." The words came out hoarse and mumbled, typical of one who hadn't spoken in days.

"You're missing the point. You are not allowed to leave this sanctuary, not at midday, not ever. If someone sees you, if the authorities catch you - they'll cut you up in thin slices and put your body parts under a microscope."

The urchin growled, more a complaint than a threat, but the spirit would have none of it. Mortaki's ghost stomped his foot and pointed at the stairs. "To bed. Now!"

Cyrus went to his room but, as usual, didn't sleep. Instead, he spent the night roaming the space between the walls. First, the boy caught one of the few remaining rats and removed its head with a single bite. Then he held the animal above his face and twisted the rodent's remains like wringing out a wet towel. The urchin caught the precious drops on his tongue, but that was only a tease, his stomach demanded more. Unfortunately, since warm food was scarce, this simple midnight snack would have to do.

Overnight, storm clouds circled the mansion and gale-force winds brought a thick blanket of snow. Gusts whistled through cracks in the foundation and the windows rattled in protest. Despite the memory of several blazing fireplaces, Mortaki's home failed to offer any warmth. Cyrus crept behind the walls and watched his master through a crack in the parlour's oak panelling. The phantom slithered over the sofa and appeared to melt into his skeletal remains. As soon as the first ghostly snores echoed through the grand hall, Cyrus scurried through the hidden maze and found his way to the pantry, where he slipped out from under the kitchen sink. A few steps later, he snuck out the back and, once again, frolicked amongst the trees.

***

It seemed a bit of snow was all it took for the village to turn on their Christmas lights. The streets below glowed in festive merriment while the sun stayed hidden from another cold night. But unfortunately, Cyrus didn't appreciate the beautiful decorations. No one had ever given him a gift as far as he could remember and unless Santa was bringing three chubby squirming piglets on a spit, the whole idea was a sham. Soon the snow started to fall again and the boy glanced at grey smoke coming out of Mortaki's many chimneys. He blinked and the illusion was gone. Going home once meant warmth, but now it only offered haunted memories of a life of confinement.

So what would become of this monstrosity, this freak of nature so alien that even the person closest to him kept him locked up and hidden? What would happen to Cyrus now that Mortaki was dead? The boy didn't know. Perhaps he wasn't even that self-aware. But he did understand something had changed and he decided to leave the familiarity of the mansion.

The boy crept through the forest to the hollow-root tree and burrowed in beside the stiff corpse of the woman he had previously dispatched. Mortaki wasn't his father, but perhaps this woman could be his mother. He pressed his lips against her frozen skin and fell asleep while considering the idea. Then, before dawn, he could no longer take the cold or stand the hunger. The woman offered neither warmth nor nourishment. Her frosted dead flesh did nothing for his appetite. He wandered down the hill.

He found a Goodwill donation bin in the corner of a parking lot, crawled inside and outfitted himself in a matching pink snowsuit, gloves and boots. Finally, the sun broke the horizon and lit the town centre for another frantic day of gift hunting.

The boy mingled amongst the horde of shoppers as they flooded the streets. Hidden speakers played *Silver Bells* and Victorian carolers raised their voices as if trying to compete. Youngsters pressed their faces against shop windows and studied the displays painstakingly arranged for just the season. Overhead, red ribbons adorned pine bough wreaths and a plastic sleigh with eight tiny reindeer hung across Main Street.

Like it or not, Christmas was in full bloom and Cyrus squinted his eyes, perhaps thinking that would help to stop the noise. Bell-ringing Santas appeared to occupy every corner. The closest smiled at the boy and then winked. Cyrus, always curious and hungry, thought the pot might contain food. A stew, perhaps and he inched closer for a look. The street corner Santa belted out his best ho-ho-ho and rang the bell again.

Cyrus looked into the pot and when he saw coins instead of meat and potatoes, he stuck out his tongue and glared at the man in the red suit.

"Hey, Merry Christmas, kid. Maybe Santa will bring you a nice spanking."

The urchin paused as if trying to comprehend and then he flashed a smile, briefly exposing his pointed yellow teeth.

Across the street, a young man handed out flyers and yelled like a carnival barker. "Don't miss our Little Players Theatrical production of A Christmas Carol, performances daily until New Year's Eve. Step right up, folks, get a coupon for 10% off. Don't forget to buy your tickets at the box office before they're all gone."

Cyrus wanted a coupon. He wanted to see what was so important, but a steady stream of traffic kept him pinned to the sidewalk. Soon a street vendor selling hotdogs attracted his attention, only to be shooed away when he couldn't produce any money.

Despite music offering tidings of joy and promising peace on earth, Cyrus was pushed and knocked about as if the shoppers didn't even see him. The boy found the back alleys less intimidating and more his style. The rank smell from a garbage can caught his attention and he ventured farther into no-man's-land only to trip over a stuffed sleeping bag. Movement caught the boy's attention and he crawled inside where he found a snoring man who reeked of spilt wine and perhaps a little squirt of urine. Cyrus smiled from ear to ear, then zipped himself inside. Maybe woken by a blast of fresh cold air, the drunk squirmed and thrashed in a futile attempt to escape.

"Bugger off," he mumbled.

The urchin removed his newly acquired pink mittens and put a filthy hand over the man's mouth. "Hush," he whispered, then used his other hand to crush the man's larynx. Cyrus's victim quickly lost consciousness and the urchin began his morning feast. Shortly after, the boy fell asleep and dreamed of Mortaki's old, wrinkled thigh, turning slowly on a rotisserie in front of the fireplace. The pink flesh sizzled and large drops of grease hissed when they fell into the flames. Soon the thigh turned black and the fire went out. Cyrus stirred, partially awake, and tried to make sense of the dream. Did he want to eat his master? His broken mind struggled with the idea and before he knew it, a church bell rang twelve times, signalling high noon.

Cyrus woke damp and covered his face. Sometime during breakfast, his meal had defecated and the stench managed to absorb every drop of breathable air. The boy peeled off the bloodstained stolen clothing, crawled from the sleeping bag and ventured into the alley wearing only his burlap rags. The mid-day sun slipped behind a cloud and fine powdered snow spun and swirled over his bare feet. He crouched and hugged himself in a desperate desire for warmth.

Slurred words from men, perhaps still drunk from the night before, carried closer from the far end of the alley. Cyrus made his retreat. He turned knobs and looked for places to hide.

An unlocked door led to a dark staircase and the boy followed it through a series of hallways and more stairs. Finally, he ended up on a platform high above the floor. A crowd below murmured and buzzed. Snippets of their conversations reached the rafters, and Cyrus strained to make out the words. Eventually the house lights dimmed and a man took centre stage. A circle of light found him and he began to speak.

"Marley was dead. That was certain. You need to believe this, or nothing wonderful can come from this story." The spotlight followed the narrator across the stage. Red velvet curtains opened to reveal Scrooge working in his office.

Cyrus watched from the darkness of the balcony. He bounced in his seat and silently clapped at the appearance of the old miser. Ebenezer reminded him of Mortaki, his master and Cyrus found Scrooge's meanness nostalgic and comforting. Sometime during the play the boy, still full and tired from overeating, fell asleep and only awoke during the final act.

Cyrus hated the ending. Ebenezer's transformation disgusted the urchin and he wanted to rip out the man's intestines. His master wasn't generous or delightful and the boy bit his own arm hard enough to draw blood, seeing him portrayed that way. The audience stood and applauded. Cyrus covered his ears and growled.

The boy waited for the happy crowd to leave and then crawled into the rafters. He swung from one joist to the next and only slipped once. His three claw-like fingernails dug into the wood while he dangled from one arm forty feet above the theatre floor. Soon he reached the edge of the tall red velvet curtains and slid to the stage.

His master was easy to spot. Even though the man faced the back, his black top hat gave him away. Cyrus screamed and once again dropped on all fours. He galloped and lunged at the unsuspecting actor. Moments later, Cyrus began his work.

The police arrived just as the boy pulled his blood-covered face away from Ebenezer's midsection. They didn't hesitate to fire and the shots ripped holes in the stage floor. Splinters stabbed at Cyrus's legs and a bullet grazed his shoulder. Bleeding now, the boy rolled offstage and disappeared in the darkness.

Outside he barely felt the cold sidewalk against his dirty black feet. The burlap rags serving as clothing did little to stop the winter's chill, but Cyrus didn't notice. He was injured and needed to get home, not to the old mansion, but to his new place amongst the roots.

Blood rolled down his arm and left a treasonous trail in the snow. The police were in pursuit, and there was nothing Cyrus could do to stop the flow. He ran through the woods, dove into his cave and held his breath. The police lingered around for half an hour before Cyrus heard them speak.

"The trail ends over there, by the old Maple."

"So, where did he go then? Up the tree?

"No, I think he doubled back and hid till we went by. I bet you a turkey dinner he's hiding somewhere in town."

"Fair enough. Let's go back and get the dogs. It's Christmas Eve and I want to spend it at home with the kids."

Cyrus smiled and started to burrow. He filled in his tunnel as he went to make sure nothing could follow.

He Knows When You're Awake

Thomas M. Malafarina

Patience wasn't among the virtues young Timmy France possessed. He was eleven years old and seemed to have even less patience than he had when he was much younger. This was especially true when it came to events like birthdays or, more importantly, Christmas.

He no longer believed in Santa Claus, his elves, or his flying reindeer, but Timmy kept this secret from his parents. He thought telling them might somehow ruin Christmas. It seemed important they thought he still believed, so he played along.

Timmy looked forward to Christmas every year, especially the presents. He loved guessing what his parents had bought for him, but hated the waiting. As soon as the gifts appeared under the tree on Christmas Eve, Timmy was ready to tear them open. His parents would never allow such a thing. They had a strict set of rules regarding the holiday. One was he had to wait until Christmas morning to open his presents.

He sometimes wondered if the reason his parents, especially his father, wanted him to believe in Santa was that it gave them one more way to make sure he did whatever they wanted. His dad would often use all the standard Christmas threats against him, such as "Bad boys get coal in their stockings" or "He sees you when you're sleeping, he knows when you're awake." As if this wasn't bad enough, for some unknown reason, his father felt the need to take these threats to a much higher and, unfortunately, much more disturbing level. Timmy had no idea why.

He remembered the first time his father had told him one of his strange tales. He had been a boy of four or five and it still bothered him to think about it.

"You know, Timmy," his father had said, "Most people only know about the good side of Santa Claus and his elves. You know how he brings toys and candy to good boys and girls."

"Yeah, I know, Daddy."

"But nobody ever talks about what happens to the bad kids, do they?" Timmy had said nothing.

Then his father asked, "Do you know what happens to bad boys and girls at Christmas time, Timmy?"

Timmy hesitated for a moment, then reluctantly said, "You told me Santa brings the bad kids coal."

"Oh no, no, Timmy. It's much, much worse than that. You see, Santa is magical. Do you know what that means?"

"Yes, Daddy, I know what magic is."

"Well, it means Santa can change into whatever sort of creature he wants to if he needs to punish a bad little boy."

"I... I don't understand, Daddy. What do you mean?"

"Well, let's say some little boy breaks one of the Christmas rules, maybe the little boy doesn't go to sleep early on Christmas Eve. You know that's one of our rules, right, Timmy?"

"Yes, Daddy."

"Well, if Santa finds out, he might turn himself into an ugly old monster then come into the boy's house and smash all his presents."

"That would be mean!" Timmy argued.

"Yes, it most certainly would be. Or maybe if the little boy was very naughty, Santa might turn his elves into trolls. You know what trolls are, don't you, Timmy."

"Yes, Daddy. They're horrible monsters."

"They sure are. And these trolls would capture the boy and carry him away to eat for dinner."

Timmy's mother had shouted at her husband, "Bob, stop that now! You'll terrify the boy!"

"Better that he be scared, Margaret, than end up in the cookpot of some horrible troll."

Timmy had been horrified by his father's story. He conjured up an image of jolly old St. Nick transforming into some kind of monstrous horned demon and his elves becoming hideous trolls.

"So, Timmy. You have to make sure you never break any of our Christmas rules. I would hate to think what Santa would do to you if you did. To make matters worse, he might take it out on your mother and me for not teaching you the rules of Christmas. You wouldn't want that, would you?"

These fear tactics had worked for several years and Timmy made a point of doing exactly as his parents told him. That was until Timmy stopped believing. Once that happened, he no longer feared demonic Santa or fanged elves. If there was no

Santa, there was no threat. However, he didn't let his parents know he was aware the tales were nothing more than a bunch of nonsense.

Now he was eleven, Timmy decided things should be different. He had formulated a plan. He'd still allow his dad to go on with his annual stories about demonic Santa and his cannibalistic elves, all the while pretending to be terrified. Then he'd wait until they were asleep and he'd slip downstairs to check out his presents. He figured he'd start with his stocking since returning it to its original state would be easiest. Most of the time, his mom just crammed stuff into the stocking with no rhyme or reason.

The wrapped gifts would be a bit trickier. He would try first to look through the paper using his flashlight to see what waited beneath. He knew some of the presents might involve his opening one end to see what was inside. He'd bring along a pair of scissors and some transparent tape. If necessary, he could always refasten the paper using his tape. His folks would never be the wiser.

Timmy lay awake in his bed on Christmas Eve, fine-tuning his plan. He waited for a full hour after his parents went to bed before going downstairs, He thought he heard a strange noise coming from his parent's bedroom. He didn't recognize the sound, but it was so unusual that it caused an icy chill to skitter down the middle of his back.

At first he thought he heard a growling noise, then a thumping sound followed by a gasp. He sat silently for several minutes, waiting to hear the noise again, but it didn't come. He thought he must have imagined it or else it was just his father tossing in his sleep. Timmy slowly opened his door and crept past his parents' bedroom.

Usually, by this time of night, he could hear his father's snoring; the man had a snore that could rattle the floorboards, but tonight he was sleeping soundlessly. His mother always slept without making a sound. Cautiously, Timmy walked down the stairs, careful to keep to the outside edges of the stair treads. He had learned this trick from a detective movie he'd watched. It was supposed to keep the steps from squeaking. He reached into his pajama pants pocket, took out his small Maglite and shone it on the area in the living room where he knew the Christmas tree stood.

On the floor, at the base of the ornately decorated tree, Timmy saw a Christmas stocking with his name embossed in raised glitter lettering. His mother had made it for him years earlier. The bottom part of the Y had worn off over the years. He had always thought it was the most beautiful stocking he'd ever seen. He remembered how she had told him Santa and his elves had made it especially for him. Seeing his stocking always made him feel special. He looked around to make sure neither of his parents had woken up or had heard him creeping about the house. He was still alone. He slowly approached his stocking and, after another glance around the room, he bent down for a closer look.

Timmy lifted the stocking and reached deep down inside, having not noticed how the bottom was darker in appearance than the rest. He was far too eager with anticipation of what he might find.

When his hand reached the toe, he suddenly got an uneasy feeling in the pit of his stomach as his fingers touched something warm, sticky and wet.

At first Timmy thought perhaps his mom had put a chocolate bar in the stockin, and it must have melted. He once had a chocolate bar melt in one of his pants pockets and it felt a lot like this. Yet this felt different, warm and unlike anything he had ever experienced before in his young life. He could feel something round and soft among the sticky wetness.

Timmy withdrew his hand and saw that his fingertips glistened with a sticky red substance with a strange coppery smell. He opened his hand, expecting to find a marshmallow based on its texture. Instead, what he saw caused a scream of unbridled terror to catch in his throat as his stomach flipped in revulsion. Sitting in the palm of his hand, floating in crimson gore, was a single human eyeball.

He jumped up, reflexively shaking his hand to rid himself of the horror, wiping it on his pajama top. He began to tremble from head to toe. He tried to scream but was unable to make a sound. Involuntary tears streamed down his face. His lips moved soundlessly as they formed a cry for his mother.

Timmy turned and ran up the stairs, taking several of them two at a time. He burst into his parents' room and stopped abruptly, staring at the bed illuminated by the moonlight shining through the window, revealing a horror beyond anything his young mind could have ever imagined. It was worse than his most graphic video game, worse than any horror movie he had ever seen.

His parents were sprawled in bed with the covers turned down. Their tattered and bloodied corpses were intensely visible against the white bed sheet, now splattered crimson. Blood had soaked their pajamas. His father's body was sitting up in bed; his throat slit from ear to ear, looking like some hideous, toothless grin. It was also evident by the gaping black hole in his skull that one of his eyes was missing. Timmy knew where that eyeball was now.

"He knows when you're awake," a deep, gruff, guttural voice hissed from a darkened corner of the bedroom. "Oh, Timmy, Timmy. You should have listened to your father. You shouldn't have broken the rules. That makes you a very bad boy, Timmy. Bad boys must pay for breaking the rules."

Timmy stared into the darkened space as a creature slowly made its way into the moonlight. The thing was about four feet tall with long ape-like arms that hung down to the floor where there were two large hands with sharp claws. It wore a tattered green suit, ripped because it could no longer fit the muscular body of the elf, which had transformed into the beast before him. The thing's bulging hair-covered muscles glistened with sweat and Timmy could smell a horrible stench coming from the monster.

"Santa is very upset with you, Timmy France, for breaking the rules. Your parents should have warned you and you should have listened. He sent us to make things right. I'm sure when Santa sees

61

the wonderful Christmas dinner we'll be bringing back with us, he'll feel a lot better about things. You'll be our gift to him, Timmy. After all, isn't giving what Christmas is all about?"

Santa's Special

Dorothy Davies

"All aboard, all aboard!"

The steam engine clanked and groaned as if anxious for its bones, ageing as they were, puffing steam into the bitter winter air, along with a cloud of very fine grit.

Doors slammed, children shrieked in excitement, parents grinned inanely, reliving their childhood vicariously through their offspring. Late arrivals scrambled for a carriage, the porter waving at them, "hurry! Hurry!"

A silver shriek from the whistle, a wave of the green flag, one last word to the driver and the wheels began to turn reluctantly, finding their grip on the gleaming rails, the engine gathering its energy and beginning its journey through the silent, frost covered countryside. The whistle screamed before the train entered a tunnel, clear warning to whatever was in the darkness to get out of the way. It began picking up speed now, swaying from side to side on every curve and bend, the wheels spelling out their own message, soonbethere soonbethere soonbethere.

Santa's Special, a fun afternoon ride on the steam trains after a tour round the Christmas display and a visit to Santa's grotto. What could be better on a cold sunny pre-Christmas afternoon?

Another scream from the whistle, another tunnel and the message of the wheels changed to beafraid beafraid beafraid...

The sunshine vanished in a heartbeat, thick ominous clouds pressed down on the countryside and rain began to fall, hammering on the roof and windows. Freakish red rain streaked the glass, found its way through gaps in the ceilings, dropped on to the passengers, so they shrieked and screamed even as the whistle did, for the rain looked like blood, smelt like blood, stained like blood.

Someone leapt for the communication cord and yanked it hard.

Even as they shrieked and screamed, the door opened and the guard stood there, holding a machete dripping in blood. He snarled, "Who pulled the cord?"

The Doll

Rie Sheridan Rose

"It's perfect!" Melody breathed, mesmerized by the figure in the shop window. "I have to get it as Tansy's Christmas present."

Peter looked at the doll and shuddered. Something about it gave him the creeps, but Tansy wasn't his kid. If Melody wanted to get the nasty old thing for her daughter, who was he to try and talk her out of it? "If you want."

The doll stood about three feet high and was dressed in the height of Victorian fashion, down to the muff which concealed her hands. Her hair was dressed in big blonde sausage curls and her eyes were a stereotypical sky blue. A slight smile curved cherry-red lips. Peter almost expected her to open her mouth and start talking in some posh accent—like something out of Dickens... but this was New York.

The doll made him very uncomfortable, but there was no talking Melody out of something she had her heart set on. And, since he had already bought her a diamond ring for Christmas, he didn't want to risk their relationship over something as silly as a toy. No matter how creepy it was.

Melody pushed open the door of the shop. A bell tinkled, announcing the presence of customers.

Peter was disappointed to hear it. If no one were working the register, perhaps Melody would lose interest and they could try somewhere else. Tansy would be just as happy with a Barbie doll…

He wasn't even sure how they had wound up in this part of town. Nothing was familiar about it. They had been on the subway, talking over the plans for the holiday—whose house would they celebrate Christmas in, where would they spend New Year's—and suddenly realized they'd missed the stop where they intended to debark. Instead, they found themselves in a totally unknown neighborhood...leave it to Melody to find the one shop open this late on a Tuesday.

The interior of the shop was dim and crowded. Floor-to-ceiling bookcases rose into shadows on both sides of a center aisle, funneling them back towards a glass counter at the rear of the store.

Incense smoke curled lazily from the mouth of a large dragon on the end of the counter, filling the small space with the scents of jasmine and sandalwood. Behind the counter hung a bead curtain separating the room from whatever mysterious environs were off-limits to the customers.

"Hello? We'd like to make a purchase please," Melody called.

"Maybe we should just go," Peter told her, hoping against hope she would just listen for once, and not argue.

"Nonsense, Peter. The doll is going to be Tansy's Christmas present and I'll hear no more about it." She turned back to the curtain. There was a service bell on the counter and Melody began pounding it with the heel of her hand. "Hello? Is anyone there? Customer..." Her voice was getting the irritated/irritating tone it got when she decided she wasn't getting the attention she deserved. He heard it a lot...

There was a shuffling sound behind the curtain and a stooped figure parted the beads with liver-spotted hands. "May I be of service?" croaked a voice as ancient as the wind.

Melody rolled her eyes and huffed in frustration. "Took you long enough. I want to buy the doll in the window." She pointed toward the front of the store as if there could be any doubt which doll she meant. As far as Peter could see, there wasn't another toy in the entire store. It wasn't the sort of shop to carry such things.

The old man nodded his head. "Of course you do."

Peter raised an eyebrow. Melody was used to being in charge of any situation she found herself in, but this fellow might just give her a run for her money. He studied the shopkeeper more closely.

He looked like a Chinese scarecrow dressed in the traditional pajama-like clothing one saw on railroad workers in old movies. It probably went over big with tourists who expected something specific in a Chinese curiosity shop... His hair was snow-white, caught back in a sleek queue reaching nearly to his waist. His face was a virtual map of wrinkles, but his eyes were piercing and ageless. Peter had the strangest feeling the stoop and age-spots were affectations the man could banish at will.

The old man glanced toward him as Melody continued to prattle on about the doll, and winked.

Peter jumped. *Extremely* disconcerting.

"I didn't see a price tag on the doll," Melody was saying. "What do you want for it?"

The old man shook his head, sighing heavily. "I do not know if I should sell her to you, Miss Melody... she is *zŭzhòu*... how do you say? Cursed."

Melody didn't even notice the man's use of her name—though Peter did. She just barked derisive laughter. "Cursed? Don't be ridiculous. Name your price." She pulled out her checkbook.

"Ah, I am most sorry, but we do not accept anything but cash at this establishment."

Melody sniffed. "Who carries cash these days?" She spun toward Peter. "What have you got in your wallet?"

He pulled it out obediently, and riffled through the contents. "I've got a twenty and three ones."

"Twenty dollars would do admirably, Mr. Livingston." The old man bowed.

Peter handed him the bill, taking care not to let his fingers brush against the other man's. He fought down the urge to wipe his hand on his coat.

He didn't like the doll, but he could tell it was worth far more than twenty dollars. Maybe the curse was real... He shook himself out of the fancy. Cursed objects weren't *real*. Not in his world.

"She is very old," the old man was telling Melody. "She is not really intended for play—especially not for a six year old. I fear if Miss Tansy treats her roughly, she will retaliate."

Melody snorted derisively, still not registering the man's uncanny knowledge. Peter felt his breath begin to catch in his throat. "W-who are you?" he whispered.

"They call me the Caretaker, Mr. Livingston. I tend the shop and its contents."

The old man turned back to Melody, but Peter could not get over the strange feeling the ancient 'Caretaker' was not what he appeared to be.

"Put it in a box," Melody ordered. "I don't suppose you gift-wrap in a place like this."

"Of course we do. I'll only be a minute." He took the doll and shuffled back into the rear environs.

Peter whirled to Melody. "C'mon—let's just go."

Her eyes widened and she sighed heavily. "You've already paid for it. I'm not leaving here without the doll."

Desperately, he played the last card he could think of. "Tansy is just going to break it—then she'll make a fuss about not getting anything for Christmas—"

"Are you worried about you precious money? I'll pay you back when we get home. Now, there's an end to it. I don't want any more argument from you!"

Peter slumped. There was no reasoning with her when she got like this. He bowed to the inevitable.

The beaded curtain rattled softly and the old man returned, carrying a beautifully wrapped box. The paper was crimson and gold and someone had added an ornate bow. On closer inspection, Peter could see the symbols on the box were Chinese characters. He wondered if they said anything coherent or were merely decorative. Another shiver ran through him. What if it were a curse? Or worse, a ward?

"Here is your purchase, Miss Melody. I hope you do not regret the choice."

Melody practically snatched the box from his hands. "Let's go home, Peter. I want to hide this before Tansy gets back from choir practice."

***

Christmas morning dawned clear and cold. Peter awoke to excited squeals from the living room. He groaned. It felt like he had only just closed his eyes. Melody had dragged them to a Christmas Eve performance of *The Nutcracker* and then to midnight mass. They weren't even Catholic.

To top it all off, when they got home, he wasn't allowed to crawl into bed until Melody was satisfied with the way each package was arranged under the tree. It had taken him hours to get it just right. The box with the ring was still hidden in his underwear drawer. He hadn't decided if he really wanted to give it to Melody or not any more.

He threw on a dressing gown and went into the living room. The scene meeting his eye looked like the aftermath of a tornado. Scraps of paper and discarded boxes were everywhere. It looked as if Tansy had glanced at each expensive gift and tossed it aside. She only had one gift left to open—the lavishly wrapped box containing the doll.

Melody knelt beside the excited child, her eyes shining. "This is a special gift just for you, baby. I hope you like it."

70

Tansy ripped the paper off, disregarding the beauty of the wrapping. She lifted the lid from the box and her face twisted with puzzlement. "Another doll?" Her voice dripped disappointment. "I don't need another doll. I wanted a Play Station." She sighed and set the box aside.

Melody reached into the box and pulled out the doll. "But this is a special doll, Tans—can't you see?" She pointed out the rich velvet clothing and the fur muff. "See how pretty her clothes are? They are what the real girls would wear in the old days. What the rich girls wore—like you might when you grow up."

Tansy snorted. "Why would I want to wear stupid skirts and a dumb hand-thingy like hers? It's way old fashioned." She reached over and picked up a handheld game console. "I'm going upstairs now." She clambered to her feet, ran to the stairs and up toward her room.

Melody sat smoothing the doll's golden curls. "I thought she'd like it," she whispered. Then she stiffened and cradled the doll in her arms. "Well, I'll just keep it for myself then." With a nod, she rose to her feet and went up the stairs herself.

Peter stared after the two of them. He wasn't surprised Tansy hadn't liked the doll. He'd tried to tell Melody as much. A frisson of distaste slips down his back. If Melody was going to keep the doll for herself... *where* was she going to keep it?

He followed Melody up the stairs with a heavy tread. He peeked around the door of their bedroom and sighed. "Are you going to put the thing in here?"

71

She turned with a smile from the dresser where she had set the doll in a place of prominence. "Doesn't she look pretty there?"

Peter bit his lip. "She's—"

"—perfect," Melody breathed.

***

When they readied for bed later, Peter found his gaze straying across the room to focus on the doll. Something about it made him want to run screaming from the bedroom and hide in the cellar.

When she had her nightgown on, Melody picked up the doll and climbed into bed.

"Are—do you seriously plan on sleeping with it?" he gasped.

"Why not?"

Peter's mind raced, seeking an excuse. "Won't you muss her clothing? And what about her hair?"

"It can be fixed," she replied stubbornly.

He plucked his pillow from the bed and rummaged in the top of the closet for a spare blanket.

"What are you doing?"

"I'm going to sleep on the couch."

Melody's eyes rolled. "Fine." She turned her back to him, cuddling the doll like it was a child.

Peter went downstairs into the living room. It was still littered with the detritus of the morning's packages and the tree lights blinked off and on in the corner, as if determined to perform its duty no matter how lame it might be.

He pulled the plug out. It would be hard enough to sleep on the lumpy couch without that damn thing flickering on and off all night. He tried to get comfortable, but his mind was endlessly churning over Melody's obsession with the doll.

What was it about the thing she found so fascinating? It was just a simpering toy…

He punched the pillow a couple of times to both make it more comfortable and relieve some of his frustration. It helped a little. He closed his eyes with a sigh, eventually falling into an uneasy sleep.

A scream jolted him awake.

What the hell?

He fought free of the tangled blanket and ran for the stairs. The screams continued, sounding more like those of a wounded animal now.

He stumbled up the stairs as quickly as he could and went first to check on Melody. He might not have given her the ring today… but he still loved her. He staggered through the doorway and stopped dead in his tracks.

The bed was a crimson lake. Melody lay on her back, sightless eyes staring at the ceiling. Her throat gaped open—slashed from ear to ear.

Peter covered his mouth in horror, holding in the scream that wanted to break free. What if he had been sleeping beside her? Who could have done something like this? Questions rattled inside his brain like marbles pinging from one wall to another.

He heard a whimper from down the hall. Tansy! She was just a kid, He had to save her.

He inched down the hall and peeked into her room.

73

Tansy cowered against the headboard, eyes threatening to pop out of her skull. She made the little whimpering noises he had heard as she stared at the figure standing in front of her.

It was the doll.

Its muff hung from the string around its neck and both hands were now exposed. They were red with blood and one held a knife which glittered in the light from the window. As he stared, aghast, its head twisted around to see him—completely backwards, like the girl in *The Exorcist*.

"She should have listened to you," it said, its voice like poisoned honey. "You both should have listened to the Caretaker. I am kept for *special* customers." It thrust the knife forward, stabbing Tansy in the heart.

Peter collapsed to his knees, broken by grief. Sobs wracked his body. He watched as the doll climbed down from the bed, its clothes no longer pristine green velvet, but soaked in blood. The pretty features were twisted into a mask of gleeful hate.

Peter closed his eyes, waiting for the inevitable.

***

The Caretaker stood in his cluttered shop. He shook his head the next morning when he found the doll standing in its usual place in the window—not a hair out of place, or a speck of dirt on its lovely Victorian costume.

"Back so soon? That's too bad. I liked Mr. Livingston. He had a good heart." He adjusted the doll's pose a touch. "He should have listened when I told him of the curse... but they never do."

The doll's smile widened.

The Children Know

Liam A. Spinage

Old Mary Pickham was the most uncharitable soul that ever did walk the gaslit streets of London. She stooped as she stepped, she swore at each chore, she hated as she waited.

It was her lot in life to be the sole caretaker of the parish orphanage and workhouse, an occupation which gave her no satisfaction in life, but which gave opportunities aplenty to inflict her own particular brand of cruelty on her charges with relish - and with very little oversight.

The children were all bundled up for Christmas Eve and 'playing' in the snow of the little courtyard at the front of the building, behind the locked iron gates which prevented them from getting ideas over their heads like running away. Usually the children of this age over which she had been granted control would be huddled up inside ragpicking, which is as unappealing a task as it sounds but one deemed by the parish to be suitable for the youngsters. Occasionally a sweep would come by and take one of the smaller boys as an apprentice, guaranteeing him a life of ashen misery and an early death. The best work for small hands was picking through rags, sorting, tiring as it was and leading to problems with eyesight when performed under the light of only three candles old Mary would permit for their use. Still, it usually kept them quiet enough that she didn't have to raise a slipper or belt to them very often, leaving her to get slowly sotted on gin as she supervised them from the little rocking chair next to the fireplace.

Occasionally one of the cursed urchins would find something interesting in the pile of rags. Then they would begin to smile and laugh among themselves, which was something that above all else old Mary could not abide. Her life had only been sorrow, pain and hardship. Why should others be allowed even a modicum of joy in theirs? When this happened, she rose in a drunken stupor and set about them with the heaviest and most punishing implements to hand - a slipper, a frying pan, a rolling pin - chasing and beating and berating them until, in fear, they relented and knuckled down again.

On this occasion, though, she had had enough of their noise altogether and banished them outside, locking the door solidly behind her. Perhaps one of them would freeze to death in the snow-filled courtyard or slip on the ice and break a bone. That would teach them, It didn't matter anyway - she couldn't hear them from where she sat. Out of sight, out of mind.

Most of the children were engaged in building a snowman in the middle of the courtyard. The eldest, Douglas, even made the joke that he would be a fine companion for old Mary, being just as cold as she was. This elicited a little laughter from the crowd so Douglas - who was on a roll now - pulled out a top hat from under his threadbare coat and placed it ceremoniously on the snowman's head, doffing his own cap when the task was done.

"Upon my word! Here is a fine gentleman to call upon our own Mary and take her away from this life of misery!" The little group of children laughed again, secure in the knowledge that Mary would probably be stone cold drunk by now or asleep in her chair.

"Where did you get that hat?" That question came from Jemima, whose perpetually grubby face was now red-cheeked from working outside in the cold yard. "It's a bit la-de-dah for our usual take."

"It came to us this morning from old man Moreton at the undertakers. Reckon as how he might have put it in the pile accidentally. But still, finders keepers! And our gentleman caller shall have only the best when he pays a visit to old Mary this evening!" Each of them agreed that in order to win over Mary, he would have to be a jolly soul indeed. They doubted such a thing was even possible. Each of them cursed her under their breath for making their wretched life even more wretched. If Mary herself was full of hate, that hate was at least equalled amongst those in her charge. They hoped something would happen that would take her away from them, whether that was a fine gentleman come to woo her or something more sinister.

Their activity was almost instantaneously broken up by the sweary shouts of their overseer telling them their soup was ready. Mary looked out at the mess they'd made in the yard and what they'd built. She cursed under her breath and decided she was too old to deal with any of this, she would make them clear it up on Christmas morning. That would teach them.

One by one they filed silently back inside, with several of them getting whacks on the backside as they passed Mary, merely for having the insolence to bring in the snow on their bare feet. Douglas reached the door but turned around briefly and bowed theatrically to the snowman in the courtyard who had given them a moment of fun amid their life of misery.

***

Mary made sure all the kids were securely locked inside for the evening and took off to the local hostelry for several hot gin toddies before returning late, swaying on her bandy legs and cussing her meagre shawl which whipped around her thin frame, buffeted by the strong wind which appeared to have come from out of nowhere. Her legs were tired and her brain addled. All she wanted to do was to sleep.

It seemed like Mary was not going to get what she wanted.

The old iron gates creaked open as she rattled the key in the hole, then clanged shut behind her as she set the chains back in place. Then, there was silence. She made her way slowly across the courtyard, resenting the cold grey air which took so much warmth from her frail form, her fate at having to perform such a duty as taking care of these unruly and unkempt young tykes and her eyesight because she swore she saw something out of the corner of her eye, movement where there shouldn't be something moving.

It came upon her suddenly, with a swift flurry of snow and a swifter flurry of fists. She recoiled from the strength of those blows but also from the chill of its touch which left great red welts swelling on her skin wherever those blows landed. In a last-ditch effort to save her wretched hide, Mary Pickham tried to scream and run toward the door, desperately working to get into the relative warmth of her workhouse quarters and away from this sudden hail of abuse. She failed at the first. She tried to call out, but her icy breath froze on her lips and sealed her mouth shut. The form continued to lope towards her, thrashing the air before it with its icy fists. Pressed against the door meant there was nothing she could do against its assault. It loomed over her, its unfeeling eyes black as coal and its breath cold as the dead of winter. It unballed its fist to reveal long fingers, each as sharp and deadly as an icicle. Then it began to rake those claws over her prone body. When it was done, it removed the top hat with a flourish and gave her a long, deep bow as the red of her blood mingled with the white of the snow and began to trickle away from the door, running pink rivulets into the grey slush accumulating at the corners of the brickwork.

The bloody pulp which was all that remained of Old Mary was discovered the next morning by a visiting tradesman, concerned that she had not replied to his many shouts from the gate. The dutiful and fastidious soul raised the alarm and summoned the local constabulary to take care of the investigation, though not before removing from the coffers 'that which was owed to me right and proper by the cantankerous old witch'.

Of her assailant, there was no trace. When the police had finished clearing the snowdrift in the workhouse courtyard, all they found was a corn cob pipe, a button and a battered top hat. Inspector Newcross picked the hat up and brushed off the light dusting of snow. He turned it over slowly in his cold fingers, looking for a name or a maker's mark written into the lining. It was a good quality item. Not something he'd expected to see in this establishment. He decided to keep it as a perk of the job.

The inspector arranged for a temporary custodian to take care of the building and the remaining orphans until the parish council could find a more permanent solution. He knew that the chances of them picking a kindly soul who actually liked children was miniscule. There was nothing here to warm his heart, just never-ending poverty and misery. He stood at the wrought iron gates awaiting their arrival, contemplating the words they had all spoken under questioning. He had never encountered such a conspiracy of silence except among the most hard-bitten criminals of the capital. There was one phrase, though, which they had all uttered in shared whispers. Damn, but it almost sounded like a veiled threat.

"He'll be back again someday."

Whatever had happened here the previous night would remain in the unsolved files of Scotland

Yard. But the Inspector was sure of one thing. The children knew.

Santa And The Cat Lady

Diane Arrelle

Santa Claus started to climb into the sleigh but was stopped by his personal valet elf, Cogswell.

"Hey, Boss, don't forget this," the elf said and sprayed Father Christmas with his special blend cologne; essence of catnip, fir tree and mistletoe.

"Ho-ho-ho!" Santa laughed and inhaled. The scent immediately made him think about Isobel.

Beautiful Isobel, the love of his life, adored the smell. She told him every year that it reminded her of the two things she loved the most, kitties and Christmas. Of course, then she'd add, "Oh and of course it reminds me of how much I love you, Nicky."

He loved it when she called him Nicky.

He suddenly stopped thinking about her and remembered where he was and where he was going. He climbed into the sleigh and said, "Thank you, Cogswell. Don't wait up; I'll be home in a few days."

Then he laughed again and, snapping the reins, began his Christmas Eve run. He'd been Santa ever since the elves recruited him back when he'd been an apprentice monk three centuries in the past. The other Santa, the one before him, never came back, something that happened every few centuries. The elves had waited the full thirty days before unlocking a glass case and opening the book of

Claus. Then, following the millennia old instructions, the elves went on the 'Santa Search' site, a magic version of the internet (which has been secretly around for as long as there has been magic) and found him.

From the moment they came for him, he had loved being the big guy, delivering joy around the world and for almost the entire last century, he had especially loved sharing his joy with his special someone. Since Isobel entered his life more than ninety years ago he didn't have to fly home exhausted after all the deliveries. Now, he had someplace to go. Since meeting Isobel he had spent every Christmas day with the love of his life and her cats.

He went to his first stop, the animal shelter, and dropped off bags of food and meds, then walked to the cat section. So many cats, meowing, purring, reaching out as he walked by them. It was always so difficult not to take them all, but he could only take one. He recalled the time he had taken all the cats and dogs from the shelter and left them under Christmas trees. He'd wondered why he hadn't thought about it before. A few weeks later half the animals went back to shelters and another thirty percent ended up neglected, tortured or dead. That left only twenty percent of all those animals loved and happy. Now he had the elves scan the naughty and nice lists and match up the children who would take care of their gift. He had a special bag just for that list and he went though it quickly, gathering the cats and dogs that were requested. The magic in the bag kept them all happy as they waited for their new hopefully forever home.

He finished quickly and then looked for the one for Isobel.

There it was, the large red tabby which stared at him with interested yellow eyes. He smiled, took the cat out of the cage and put it in his carrier. He placed the 'thank you' card with the hundred-dollar bill in her now empty wire cage and, with the cat up front with him, took it along for the ride.

"Well, kitty," he said. "Isobel is going to love you. You are so big and healthy-looking and she adores red tabbies even more than calicoes."

The cat remained silent, not a mew, not a purr. It just stared at him to the point it was creeping him out and being a three-hundred-year-old man, Santa didn't get weirded out very often. "OK, kitty, here's the deal. Isobel is my lady and I give her a cat every Christmas. It's a great gig for you. She lives in a big house I got for her when we started dating. It's far away from everyone and it's surrounded by my magic. You guys get to quadruple your life span in comfort and security with a fine lady who loves each and every one of you. So lighten up and enjoy this ride."

The cat just stared at Santa in silence.

After the last package was placed by the chimney with care, Santa headed to the house in the woods. He remembered meeting Isobel with her soft, blond curls and huge blue eyes when she was eighteen. She had stayed awake just to meet him and give him a kiss. A thank you, she'd explained, for being so wonderful. And now, ninety-four years later, they were still together. He couldn't make her live an almost endless life like he did, so she aged slowly instead. But he didn't care how she grew older, he thought she was even lovelier with every new wrinkle and her hair had long ago turned white; a side effect of his magic.

He parked the sleigh on the roof and, holding the cat carrier, effortlessly slid down the chimney. He'd left Isobel's other presents and a year's supply of kitty kibble back in the sleigh. He knew he'd have plenty of time later to get them. First things first, Isobel needed to meet her new cat.

As always, just for a brief moment, he wished he could stay here forever when he entered the familiar living room. but this time he quickly noticed something was wrong.

Where was Isobel?

She was always there to greet him. "Isobel? Darling?"

No answer, then the cats began following the sound of his voice. The one in the carrier started yowling and he absently let it out to join the others. The room filled with crying felines and he noticed how underfed they were. They all looked like they were dying.

"Isobel!" he yelled, panic weighing on his chest, making it hard to take a breath. "Isobel, where are you? Answer me!"

The only sound that answered him was the increasing volume of cat cries.

He started to push through the cats when one of them bit him, hard. He looked down and found the newest cat at his feet, blood on its little fangs. He kicked the orange tabby and was immediately overwhelmed with shame. "Oh I'm so sorry," he gasped and bent to pet her. The cat swiped its claw out and scratched his face.

Santa, who was pretty close to immortal, jumped up and backwards, shocked by the pain. He couldn't remember the last time he'd felt hurt. He stumbled, stood, touched his mitten to his cheek. It came away smeared with blood. He stood, his legs shaking for a moment as he stared down the Tabby.

The cat blinked, almost as if it had lost interest, turned and left the room. Santa too turned away, then looked back at the retreating feline. He shook his head and yelled, Isobel!" No answer. He hurried from the living room in search of his mistress. He went out into the entryway and found her almost immediately… at the bottom of the stairs in the hall.

He felt like his whole world was collapsing around him, his stomach cramped up and he retched. The tears on his cheeks burned the claw marks, but he didn't even notice. He moaned, a long low cried of agony, because he realized immediately that Isobel was dead. He knew there was no mistake, no hope of being mistaken. He saw her broken legs and knew she'd fallen down the stairs.

His knees gave out and he sank to the floor… next to what was left of her. He shivered and his teeth chattered in shock because Isobel was a skeleton.

One cat that hadn't joined the others earlier was gnawing on her bony hand.

"Oh Isobel," he groaned, "How could they do this to you! My poor darling."

He felt an emotion he hadn't experienced in three centuries. Anger, no, fury. She'd loved those cats, each and every one of them and they ate her! Blindly, in a red rage, he hit the gnawing cat away, swept up her up and rocking back and forth, hugged what was left of her.

He cried tears of grief he hadn't know he could feel. "Oh, what have they done? Did they even wait until you died to do this?"

As if in answer, all the cats filed into the hallway with the red tabby in the lead. The other cats followed, allowing her to be the alpha cat. She meowed and, like magic, the rest surrounded him. He saw the hunger in their faces. They were beyond starving; Isobel must have died months ago. He realized the cats should be dead, but his magic had kept them alive and suffering. The pain these poor cats had to live with was all his fault.

They closed in on him, covering him waist deep, hemming him in and he realized he couldn't get away. He knew he wasn't immortal and would die but he was Santa; it was his obligation to help all creatures in need, especially at Christmas. He steeled himself against what would be coming and knew he would be sacrificing himself. He knew his duty and didn't shove them away when the red tabby led the final attack. The pain was awful but not as awful as the pain of losing Isobel. He felt a small solace that once he was dead the magic would die as well and hopefully the cats would be able to break out of there.

He felt the teeth tearing and shredding his arms and legs and he screamed. When they went for his eyes, he wished he were already dead and with his last ounce of reasoning wondered how long it would take for the elves to realize he wasn't coming back.

This Final Christmas Day

Rie Sheridan Rose

"Jingle Bells, Jingle Bells"—
Hear the children sing…
Don't you know it's Christmas?
We must to tradition cling…

Though a zombie ate ol' Santa,
And the reindeer all are toast…
It's still Happy Yuletide,
According to the Post.

Might as well get comfy,
The world is acting strange.
The ice caps all are melting,
And Cerberus has mange...

Bombs in crowds of children,
Weather on the fritz,
Politicians vying for which
One is biggest ditz…

We're stuck here with each other.
We can't go visit friends.
We've eaten all the fruit cakes,
And done a movie binge.

The Apocalypse is coming,

I heard the angels say…
Let's raise one last eggnog
On this final Christmas Day!

Meet the Authors

Dan Allen is Canadian and enjoys spending time in Northern Ontario. You can find his short stories in numerous magazines, anthologies and podcasts. Visit www.danallenhorror.com to see a presentation of his published work.

His terrifying look at Alzheimer's, "Above the Ceiling," is featured in Bards and Sages collection of the Best Indie Speculative Fiction Vol. 2.

A personal favourite, "Sympathy for the Zingara," can be found in the March 2019 edition of ParAbnormal Magazine.

His terrifying story, "The Basement" (edited by Horror Zine's Jeani Rector), was published by Hellbound Books in July 2020.

You can visit Dan at www.danallenhorror.com

Diane Arrelle has more than 350 short stories published and two short story collections: Just A Drop In The Cup and Seasons On The Dark Side. She, her sane husband and insane cat live on the edge of the New Jersey (USA) Pine Barrens (home of the Jersey Devil).

Dorothy Davies is an editor, writer and medium. Somehow all these things come together in her seemingly crowded leisure and work life. She retired from editing for a while to run a second hand shop, the best one on the Isle of Wight, but the thrill of finding and publishing outstanding stories became too much so she started again with the

Gravestone Press imprint. She still runs the shop... Her book, The Skullface Chronicles, the story of a zombie taking revenge on his dysfunctional family, is available through fiction4all.com. She has a store of short stories, some of which are finding their way into the anthologies, having not seen daylight for many a long year. She also channels books from spirit authors, notable figures from our history. These can be found on the fiction4all.site under Zadkiel Publishing.

Thomas   M.   Malafarina (www.ThomasMMalafarina.com) is a horror fiction author from Berks County, Pennsylvania.

To date, he has published eight horror novels *What Waits Beneath, Burner, From The Dark, Circle Of Blood, Dead Kill Book 1: The Ridge of Death, Dead Kill Book 2: The Ridge Of Change, Dead Kill Book 3: The Ridge Of War* and *Death Bringer Jones, Zombie Slayer Volume 1.* He has published seven collections of horror short stories; *Thirteen Deadly Endings, Ghost Shadows, Horror Classics, Undead Living, Malaformed Realities Vol. 1, Vol. 2, Vol. 3, Vol. 4, Vol. 5* and most recently *Vol. 6. Volumes 7* and *8* to be released in the near future. He has also published a book of often-strange single-panel cartoons called *Yes I Smelled It Too; Cartoons For The Slightly Off Center* and will soon publish *Yes I Smelled It 2: More Cartoons For The Slightly Off Center.* All of his books are published through Hellbender Books, an imprint of Sunbury Press.(www.Sunburypress.com).

Thomas' cartoons have also appeared in Twisted Pulp Magazine and he has published two cartoon books, "Charles" and "Charles: Remember To Dismember" through Screaming Eye Press.

In addition, Thomas' stories have appeared in more than 170 anthologies and e-magazines. Some have been produced and presented for internet podcasts and radio plays as well. He has shared anthology pages with some of the biggest names in horror fiction.

Thomas is also an artist, musician, singer and songwriter.

Rie Sheridan Rose multitasks. A lot. Her short stories appear in numerous anthologies, including Killing It Softly Vol. 1 & 2, Hides the Dark Tower, Dark Divinations and On Fire. She has authored twelve novels, six poetry chapbooks and lyrics for dozens of songs. She is also editor-in-chief for Mocha Memoirs Press and editor for the Thirteen O' Clock imprint of Horrified Press. She tweets as @RieSheridanRose.

Liam A. Spinage is a former philosophy student, former archaeology educator and former police clerk who spends most of his spare time on the beach gazing up at the sky and across the sea while his imagination runs riot.

David Turnbull is a member of the Clockhouse London group of genre writers. He writes mainly short fiction and has had numerous short stories published in magazines and anthologies. His stories have previously been featured at Liars League London events and read at other live events such as Solstice Shorts and Virtual Futures. He was born in Scotland, but now lives in the Catford area of London. He can be found at www.tumsh.co.uk.